Axel Scheffler & Frantz Wittkamp

HAPPY BUNNIES

English translation by Alison Green

ALISON GREEN BOOKS

Happy bunnies love to play.
Come and join our games today!

On sunny days, we race outside,
Running, jumping, keeping busy.
Some of us do somersaults.
We roly-poly till we're dizzy.

When little birds flap round our heads
It makes us dream of flying, too.
If only we could grow some wings!
We'd swoop off, soaring through the blue.

You'd think that when a rabbit sings
The sound would be quite sweet – but, no!
We sing out really loud and strong,
And sound just like a squawking crow!

Look who's here – the Easter Bunny!
Chickens come and join the queue,
To watch him decorate their eggs
With pretty colours, red, green, blue.

This funny rabbit lives alone.
He says it's peaceful out at sea.
But still, it's nice when someone calls,
And chats with him beneath his tree.

When bunnies fall in love, they say,
"I love your ears. Your whiskers, too!
My bunny-love, please marry me!
We'll be so happy, me and you."

While walking through the hills and fields,
Old Papa Rabbit waits for hours,
Leaning on his walking stick
While Mrs Rabbit gathers flowers.

Daddy Rabbit's an inventor.
Look! He's made a new TV!
I wonder what we'll watch tonight?
I hope there's something good to see!

We little bunnies love our books.
(Our dad prefers to read the news.)
Stories, poems, books of facts!
It's hard deciding what to choose.

It's hot today – let's have a swim!
We splash and play and, when we're done,
We stretch out on the soft, green grass.
(Our fur dries quickly in the sun.)

These two friends have walkie-talkies.
They're always playing secret games.
They make each other laugh a lot
And give each other silly names.

One, two, three – let's have a race!
Quick as the wind, we almost fly!
(But if we tumble with a bump,
It's fine to have a little cry.)

Someone's eaten Mummy's carrot.
"Little Bunny, was it you?"
"No! I never!" Bunny says.
Is that a fib? Or is it true?

Night is falling. All is quiet.
What does Grandpa Rabbit need?
His glasses and a little lamp –
And his favourite book to read.

The sky is dark, the stars are out,
There's still a long walk home ahead.
It's much too late to play a game.
It's time all bunnies went to bed.

The moon is smiling, round and bright.
Sweet dreams, rabbits! All sleep tight!

Published in the UK by Alison Green Books, 2022
An imprint of Scholastic
Euston House, 24 Eversholt Street, London, NW1 1DB
Scholastic Ireland, 89E Lagan Road, Dublin Industrial Estate, Glasnevin, Dublin, D11 HP5F

SCHOLASTIC and associated logos are trademarks and/or
registered trademarks of Scholastic Inc.

Based on *Wenn Hasen Gute Laune Haben*, the original picture book by Frantz Wittkamp and Axel Scheffler, first published in Germany by Beltz & Gelberg

ISBN : 978 0 702307 87 4

A CIP catalogue record for this book is available from the British Library.

Printed in China
Paper made from wood grown in sustainable forests and other controlled sources.

1 3 5 7 9 10 8 6 4 2

www.scholastic.co.uk